THE CONCOURS CAPER

E. ROBERT BROOKS

Also by E. Robert Brooks
Pirouette
Wine Thief
Derailed Gears

Publishing Coordinator – Sharon Kizziah-Holmes
Cover Design – Jaycee DeLorenzo

ISBN -13: ISBN -13: 978-1-951772-70-3

ACKNOWLEDGMENTS

Sharon Kizziah-Holmes- Publishing coordinator extraordinaire! My sincere thanks for your guidance and infinite patience as I have attempted to navigate the labyrinthic process of writing coherent stories, and for your introduction to-a talented illustrator who possesses the uncanny ability to take combinations of abstract concepts and effectively craft them into compelling imagery.

Jaycee DeLorenzo- Judging from Jaycee's illustrations, a picture really is worth a thousand words! I don't know how she always manages to so accurately interpret my notes and translate them into images that convincingly convey the themes of my plots, but I am very fortunate to have access to such talent!

PROLOGUE

The Pledge

Shortly after the United States entered the Second World War, two non-commissioned army officers from Chicago were conscripted as agents into the newly formed Counter-Intelligence Corps (CIC).

They were appointed to the American

Expeditionary Force in France and acted as insurgents to disrupt the infrastructure for the port city of Bordeaux.

During one of their missions they took shelter in an abandoned cellar during a bombing attack.

Fortuitously, their shared love of wine began that afternoon.

While huddled together in dim candlelight, they discovered old dust covered bottles which they opened and imbibed as they listened to the explosions above them.

The walls violently shook with each detonation and dust filled the air making it difficult to breathe.

Nonetheless, over the course of several hours they thoroughly enjoyed the impromptu tasting.

As they sipped and savored the wine, both because of its alluring flavor, and with the realization that each swallow might be their last taste of life, they made a pact.

If they survived the night, and the

remainder of the conflict, they would learn more about fine wine.

When they returned home after the war, they kept in touch and helped each other build prosperous businesses.

Now they planned to revisit Europe together on a lavish vacation to celebrate their success.

At a black-tie wine tasting dinner at the posh Everglades Club in Palm Beach they hatched a plan.

They agreed a gentlemanly wager for a rare magnum large format bottle of 1945 Chateau Mouton-Rothschild as the prize!

The contest, which would take place over the course of sixty days, would determine which of them could best covertly embarrass an affluent cad that they both abhorred!

The subject of this surreptitious operation was a haughty former French army officer named Guillaume Fouquet.

They had been introduced to Fouquet at military briefings in London during the war when he was attached to General

Charles de Gaulle's retinue.

He was the scion of an aristocratic family from the Loire Valley, and an instructor for the elite *Cadre Noir* cavalry corps at the prestigious military equestrian academy - *École Nationale d'Équitation,* located in the town of Saumur.

In their estimation, he was a malefactor who had dishonorably taken advantage of an impressionable young nurse when she was serving in field hospitals near the location where they had been billeted.

She subsequently fell on hard times due to her unrequited love when Fouquet jilted her.

Their intention was for this mission of revenge against Fouquet to be a noble endeavor, and the tactics were to be non-violent and subtle, with a comedic and embarrassing effect.

Their "marching orders" would adhere to- *no harm, no foul,* a term coined that year in the context of the sport of basketball when a referee decided not to call a foul because the contact was not serious enough to affect the outcome of the game.

As with their previous assignments during the war, the ends would justify the means!

Rather than just contribute to another charitable cause, they chose this somewhat novel scheme to privately commemorate the achievement of their financial fortunes, and to relive their experience as spies with this clandestine good deed.

Revenge for the wronged lady, and comeuppance for the effete Frenchman who they despised!

They would have some laughs at their nemesis' expense, and exorcize their long-standing vendetta against him…

CHAPTER ONE

The Training

In January of 1941, the office of the Chief of the Corps of Intelligence Police-Sub-Section - Investigating Section - Counter-Intelligence Branch - Military Intelligence Division, was established.

On the 24th of February, the Corps of Intelligence Police Investigators School became operational in the Army War College, and it was moved to Chicago.

On December 13th, a letter from the office of The Adjutant General officially changed the name of the Corps of Intelligence Police, to the Counter-Intelligence Corps, effective the 1st of January 1942.

Chicago natives, First Sergeant Gregory Lockwood and Corporal Kevin Dunning, who were serving in the Enlisted Reserve Corps, were ordered to overseas active duty.

They were assigned as special agents in the European theater of operation.

After completing accelerated training in communications, sabotage and demolitions, they flew to Great Britain to liaise with the British Secret Intelligence Service (SIS), also known as MI6, who infiltrated them into the fishing port of Biarritz, a tourist resort town in the French Basque country located thirty-five *kilometres* from the Spanish border.

Their mission was to gather

intelligence on the operations of the nearby U-boat base in the harbor of the city of Bordeaux, and to disrupt the Nazi naval command and control, whenever, and wherever possible.

CHAPTER TWO

The Insult

After blowing up the submarine pens in Bordeaux, Lockwood and Dunning succeeded to evade pursuit and return to London, escaping in the dead of night in a small fishing skiff.

They first met Fouquet when they were attending an intelligence briefing in advance of the invasion of Normandy.

Prior to the landing, they were assigned to parachute in with a group of commandos to sabotage the German communications infrastructure.

Fouquet was serving as the *aide-de-camp* to General Charles de Gaulle, leader of the Free French Forces in exile.

Fouquet was loudly dismissive and condescending to these junior American officers, referring to them as, "amateur saboteurs!"

By the time the orientation had concluded, Lockwood and Dunning had experienced more than enough of the unbearable Fouquet!

Their negative impression of this imperious Frenchman was exacerbated that evening when they chanced to encounter him chatting up an attractive nurse in a local pub.

It was evident that this impressionable, and somewhat inebriated woman was being hoodwinked, and that she was smitten by the suave Fouquet.

As the two soldiers shared a look of

apprehension, they finished their beers and departed.

Over the course of the next several days, they saw Fouquet with the young nurse several more times, and it was obvious that she was giddy from Fouquet's infatuation.

On the evening prior to their relocation to a Royal Air Force (RAF) base where they would be deployed, the two American soldiers returned to the pub for a last drink, only to find the nurse sitting alone in a corner drowning her sorrows in abject misery.

Taking pity on her plight, they invited her to join them for a drink.

After imbibing a dram of strong Islay single malt Scotch whisky, with tears in her eyes she explained that Fouquet had suddenly departed London without so much as a polite farewell…

CHAPTER THREE

The Objective

The *Rallye Automobile-de-Monte Carlo*, which is regarded as the most famous automotive rally in the world, was conceived in 1911.

It is a race over public roads, traditionally held each year in January.

It was originally devised for production

automobiles, as opposed to one-off specials or purpose-built race cars.

It is run by the *Automobile Club-de-Monaco*, which also organizes the Monaco Grand Prix Formula One race, as well as, in modern times, the *Rallye Monte Carlo Historique*.

In its original form, competitors would depart from random far-flung locations, with Monaco designated as the destination.

Points were awarded based on the distance traveled and the difficulty of the journey.

After World War II, when the Rally eventually resumed in 1949, the format changed, and a specific route was mandated with Monte Carlo as the start and finish of the race, and Amsterdam as the half-way point.

A *Circuit Montagne* (mountain circuit) section was added to the course.

Over the ensuing years, the route evolved and became increasingly difficult.

For the 1956 race, the infamous Alpine Col-de-Turini pass was included.

In this new iteration, private participants were gradually supplanted by factory sponsored teams.

In 1956, the Jaguars which dominated the competition that year had been previously campaigned by the Jaguar factory.

So, in principle, 1955 was the last year that traditional privateers won the race.

The Delahaye automotive manufacturing company, famed for its production of both racing and grand touring motorcars, was founded by Émile Delahaye, in 1894.

Delahaye was from the city of Tours in the Loire Valley of France, where the resident landed gentry included Guillaume Fouquet's family, who produced Vouvray wine from Chenin Blanc grapes at their estate.

At the 1951 Monte Carlo Rallye, Delahaye enjoyed a strong result.

Out of an unusually large group of one hundred competitors, Delahaye took 1st, and 5th places with their Type 175 S models, as well as 11th, and 28th places with Type 135s.

Delahaye's racing swansong was with a Type 235 that finished in eleventh place at the 23rd Monte Carlo Rallye in 1953.

The company had been suffering a dramatic decline in sales for several years, and their car production shut down in 1954.

Despite several attempts to restructure and salvage the business, the brand was gone forever by 1956.

Taking advantage of their desperate financial situation, Fouquet purchased from them for a pittance the 1953 Type 235 which had raced at Monte Carlo - the last of their factory saloon race cars.

This desirable example featured a body designed and crafted by the famed coachbuilder Henri Chapron.

CHAPTER FOUR

The Engagement

The Pebble Beach *Concours d'Elegance* is considered by automotive cognoscenti to be the most prestigious classic car show in America.

It was founded in 1950 as a complimentary event to the Pebble Beach

Road Race, an event sponsored by the Sports Car Club of America (SCCA).

The initial route for the race was orchestrated over a closed circuit of public roads.

Due to a fatality in the 1956 competition when a driver went off course and crashed into a tree, the 1957 race venue was changed to the newly built Laguna Seca Raceway (now called the Mazda Raceway).

American racing icon Phil Hill won the Pebble Beach Del Monte trophy three times (1950, 1953, 1955), and racer and legendary designer Carroll Shelby won it in 1956 - the last year of the street course.

For the first two years, the Concours was held on the grounds of the Hotel Del Monte next to the Beach Club, a private club near the Del Monte Lodge (which became The Lodge at Pebble Beach).

In 1952, the still nascent event was moved to the lawn between the Lodge and the Pacific Ocean overlooking scenic Carmel Bay.

In the contiguous Del Monte Forest, which was originally part of the Hotel Del Monte resort property, there was an area of upscale homes with an equestrian facility for the residents' horses.

The stable, known as the Pebble Beach Equestrian Center, was located near the start/finish line of the road race route on Portola Road.

It was managed by an accomplished horseman named Richard Collins, who was an eventing rider and instructor.

As a youth, Collins had graduated from a Southern California military school that had an extensive equestrian curriculum.

He was employed to head the resort's riding program in 1941 (then known as the Pebble Beach Stables), but before he could begin his duties the United States entered World War II, and he enlisted.

During his tour of duty in France, he met, and served with Sergeant Lockwood and Corporal Dunning,

After the war, he returned to Pebble Beach and assumed the management of the stables, which were renamed as the Pebble Beach Equestrian Center.

Collins put Pebble Beach on the map as one of the pre-eminent equestrian facilities in America.

He coached the United States Equestrian Team's (USET) three-day eventing squad at the 1955 Pan-American Games in Chicago.

While there, he looked up and reconnected with Lockwood and Dunning.

When he met them for dinner, knowing that they were motorcar enthusiasts Collins invited them to visit him for the 1956 Pebble Beach race and concours.

The next day, Lockwood and Dunning joined Collins at the showgrounds for the stadium jumping phase of the competition.

Of all the people Lockwood and Dunning never expected to see at this event, or wanted to ever cross paths with again, Fouquet appeared before them during their lunch break…

He was attending the games as the *chef d'équipe* (manager) for the French team, and he was as verbose and rude as ever!

As Lockwood and Dunning grimaced, Collins, unaware of their previous run-in with Fouquet, and upon learning that Fouquet was an aficionado of exceptional automobiles, invited him to also attend the next year's concours, and to visit his stables.

He was excited when Fouquet proposed to bring and exhibit his rare Delahaye motorcar, and Collins promised to use his contacts to secure an exhibitor invitation for him…

CHAPTER FIVE

The Premise

A t the former Del Monte hotel, which had been acquired by the American Navy after the war and repurposed as the Naval Postgraduate School (NPS), Lockwood and Dunning had a contact who they had "worked with" during their military service in France when they carried out commando operations prior to the amphibious invasion of Normandy.

John Baldwin had been the first Officer in Charge (OIC) of administration at NPS in Monterey.

He also served as adjutant to Rear Admiral Ernest Edward Herrmann, who was the first commanding officer of the school at its new location.

Herrmann and Baldwin had supervised the school's relocation from the United States Naval Academy in Annapolis, Maryland, to California, and Herrmann was the school superintendent from 1950 to 1952.

On November 19th, 1952, for no apparent reason, at fifty-six years of age Herrmann committed suicide with his service revolver.

Upon hearing the shot, Baldwin rushed into Herrmann's office and found him dead.

The main building of the school, which houses the principal administrative offices, was renamed in Herrmann's honor as

Herrmann Hall at a ceremony in 1956.

Baldwin relinquished his administrative duties, but he remained at the school and became an instructor.

When Lockwood phoned Baldwin and proposed that he assist them at the concours with their plot to embarrass Fouquet, he found a most willing confederate!

CHAPTER SIX

The Operation

Sergeant Gregory Lockwood walked with a pronounced limp - legacy of a shrapnel wound he had sustained during his military service.

Eschewing prescription pain medicine, he opted, instead, for copious consumption of aged fine French brandy to ameliorate his frequent bouts of pain.

For the first phase of their mission, Lockwood took the lead and devised the initial trial of the contest.

His plan was to use intermediaries to facilitate many of the preparations and all of the overt actions.

He and Dunning would make the effort to be overly polite and obsequious to Fouquet so that it would never occur to him that they had been involved in his trials and tribulations.

They would make sure to be seen with Collins and Fouquet for all the event activities - joining them for the tour of the stables, the race, at several dinners and for breakfast on the morning of the concours, as well as for the judging afterwards.

The plan encompassed several elements that would need to be executed with military precision.

It was essential that the sequence of events adhere to Lockwood's exacting schedule so that cumulatively they would have the desired effect.

Fouquet had arranged to ship his Delahaye well in advance of the Pebble Beach Concours.

It would be securely stored up until the morning of the judging.

There would be a brief window of opportunity when the car was transported to the showgrounds to make the "improvements" that Lockwood had contemplated.

At Lockwood's request, Baldwin had arranged for the driver of the transport truck to be a navy mechanic who owed him a favor because he had helped get his son accepted to the NPS.

The plan was to quickly remove key accessories from the motor, substituting them with similar-looking parts that to the eyes of a discerning specialist would be identified as non-original.

The lack of originality would result in a lower score, that, despite the claimed and well-documented excellent provenance, would preclude Fouquet's car from winning its class.

To assure that outcome, through well-placed innuendos questioning the authenticity of Fouquet's entry Baldwin had also prevailed upon a Delahaye "marque authority", who would be attending as a judge, to make sure to catch any inconsistencies in the presentation of the car.

The other judges would defer to the specialist's opinion as the recognized expert.

The second technique they would use to upset Fouquet involved caustic battery acid.

The sulfuric acid used in car batteries is a skin irritant that can damage clothing.

Especially when the fabric is made from cotton.

At Baldwin's behest, one of his subordinate staff would be carrying a small spray bottle of this potent acid.

Unawares to Fouquet, this *provocateur* would stealthily spatter some of the acid on the back of Fouquet's suit that morning.

By the afternoon, after being exposed

to the bright sunlight all day the fabric should become discolored, and might even develop small holes and Fouquet's skin would likely become quite irritated!

CHAPTER SEVEN

The Sortie

After sharing a hearty breakfast, Lockwood and Dunning accompanied Collins and Fouquet to the lawn where the entrants for the concours had been staged in preparation for the judging.

As they were leaving the restaurant, a

waiter bumped into Fouquet and apologized profusely to the indignant Frenchman.

Lockwood and Dunning observed the waiter successfully spray the back of Fouquet's jacket with the acid as he flashed them a conspiratorial wink.

Collins and Fouquet had carefully attired themselves for the event, with Collins wearing a corduroy jacket with suede patches on the elbows and a tweed riding cap, and Fouquet sporting a fawn-colored houndstooth jacket with a burgundy ascot insolently worn around his neck within his shirt collar.

Lockwood and Dunning had also dressed for the occasion, with Lockwood looking very ivy league in his seersucker suit and bow tie, and Dunning opting for a khaki suit with a doe skin vest and classic Bucks shoes.

Fouquet's Delahaye had been painstakingly detailed and it looked impeccable.

It was a shame that he was fated to lose

the prize which he so shamelessly coveted!

Over the next several hours, nattily dressed spectators milled around the grounds.

Two judges, who were attired in white lab coats looked over the Delahaye and seemed to be duly impressed as they discussed and evaluated it in hushed voices.

Based on Fouquet's assessment of the judges' opinions, he exuded smug confidence that he would be awarded the best of show trophy!

The next official inspector to approach them was the marque specialist for French motorcars.

A man of large proportions, he wore a jaunty Fedora hat and his loud and imperious voice resonated as he shared his insights about the ill-fated history of the Delahaye company.

The specialist asked Fouquet several questions to verify the unique provenance.

Initially, this expert seemed to be just as impressed with the presentation as the previous judges.

However, as he looked closely under the bonnet he began shaking his head and making disapproving noises...

Alarmed, Fouquet confronted him about why he was indicating concern?

The judge proceeded to admonish Fouquet, pointing out several incorrect parts including an air cleaner that was clearly a Dodge product and a steering rack that was from a Jaguar.

Fouquet, never one to accept criticism graciously accused the judge of being an imbecile!

When Fouquet rounded on him, the judge noticed that the back of Fouquet's jacket was discolored and perforated with myriad small ragged holes, and he retorted that the Frenchman's clothing was just as shabby as his car!

As Fouquet fumed at the insult, the judge tore up his score sheet, turned, and stalked away...

Though they were exuberant at the success of their plan, the two former spies had been well-schooled about how to hide their inner thoughts and they maintained deadpan expressions.

They offered Fouquet polite condolences for his misfortune, and revealed nothing of their complicity as they listened to his irate tirade.

As a growing group of amused spectators looked on, a thoroughly dejected Fouquet removed his jacket, went down to the water's edge and threw it into the ocean…

The compatriots agreed that Lockwood had scored a resounding success in their competition.

Now it was up to Dunning to raise the bar and create an even more scurrilous situation to embarrass Fouquet!

CHAPTER EIGHT

The Skirmish

After spending several days meandering through Normandy in their rented Peugeot, followed by a week reminiscing in Bordeaux, the two conspirators traveled to the Loire Valley for the next leg of their "vacation."

Corporal Kevin Dunning had grown up

on a farm outside of Rock Island, Illinois.

His father had worked as an engineer for the International Harvester farm equipment company.

From an early age, Dunning had learned machinery repair skills so that he could help his father maintain the equipment on their farm.

Dunning discovered that he had an instinctive ability to understand mechanical design.

He would later use this aptitude to develop bomb-making skills during the war.

It quickly became evident to Lockwood that Dunning had indeed prepared a suitable scenario to increase Fouquet's discomfiture!

Courtesy of a British contact at MI5 named Peter Wright who had administered their communications training in London prior to their wartime assignment in France, Dunning was in possession of a sophisticated miniature surveillance listening device - codenamed SATYR, which was based on a design that the Russians had developed at the end of the war.

With its diminutive size, and constructed with a passive cavity resonator with no power supply or active electronic components, the device was virtually impossible to detect.

Dunning bribed a disgruntled worker - the winery cellarmaster at Fouquet's chateau - to plant this bug in Fouquet's office.

Using a discreet radio transmitter tuned to the specific frequency to activate the resonator, Dunning listened in on Fouquet's meetings and phone conversations.

Dunning had learned that Fouquet had scheduled a visit to his chateau for a group of American importers to sample his Vouvray wines.

Dunning then paid his mole handsomely to move the bug to the tasting room prior to the event, and to contaminate the wines.

The plan was that the winemaker would quit immediately after the tasting.

Dunning had arranged employment for him at another winery.

Fouquet was elated! He had received the final confirmation of his reservation to exhibit his Delahaye at the end of May at the *Concours d'Élégance Villa d'Este*.

In the meantime, he was confident that he would charm his gullible American visitors and easily convince them to purchase a large quantity of his wines.

Their initial payment to him would be just in time to cover his costs for participating in the concours.

As a titled landowner, with more property then cashflow, beneath his pretentious aristocratic veneer Fouquet was often scrambling to maintain his lavish lifestyle.

Upon the arrival of his American guests, and after showing them the equestrian facilities where his *Selle Francais* show horses were trained, Fouquet adjourned with them to the tasting room at his adjacent winery.

While Fouquet had been conducting the stable tour, the winemaker had chilled and opened all the samples.

As Fouquet and the winemaker poured the wines, Fouquet explained in glowing terms how his Chenin Blanc grapes were cultivated and harvested.

Dunning's accomplice had told him that he felt certain that Fouquet would assume that the wines had already been checked to verify that they were sound.

Fouquet would not bother to double-check this before pouring them.

The cellarmaster confirmed to Dunning that he had adulterated the samples just as he had promised.

The tasters' reactions, which were recorded through the listening device, were priceless!

One of them remarked that all the samples had a strong aroma of cat pee and sulfur, and the other participants agreed, talking amongst themselves that these wines were obviously flawed...

Fouquet's contrived veneer of genteel civility instantly vanished, and he brashly accused his guests of not knowing what they were talking about!

Then, upon sampling the wines, he belatedly realized to his astonishment that they were in fact unpalatable.

He confronted his winemaker, loudly accusing him of incompetence!

Before Fouquet could have the satisfaction of summarily firing him on the spot, the winemaker called him a *salop* and announced that because of Fouquet's arrogance and stupidity, that this was the worst managed winery in the entire Loire Valley region, and that he quit!

Fouquet was apoplectic! For perhaps the first time in his life he was speechless...

Wordlessly, he watched as the winemaker and his guests, shaking their heads, walked out on him...

As the reel-to-reel tape recorder (a German invention) captured the verbal banter, Lockwood and Dunning were doubled over with laughter!

After they caught their breaths, they toasted Dunning's success with some of the untainted Vouvray that the winemaker had given to Dunning.

The bouquet was reminiscent of fresh peaches, and the refreshing flavor balanced by bracing acidity was really quite good!

Lockwood stood and raised his glass to Dunning, acknowledging that this round of the competition was a resounding success for his former military subordinate!

CHAPTER NINE

The Interlude

From the Loire Valley, en route to Italy the two Americans sojourned to the French Riviera, known as the *Cote d'Azur*, for a quick stay at the Hotel Negresco in Nice.

They enjoyed a sumptuous dinner at the hotel's famed restaurant *Le Chantecler*.

The grand old hotel had seen better days and it would be sold the following year, but it still retained signs of its former glory.

Noteworthy architectural features included an immense Baccarat chandelier and its prominent pink dome.

The regional menu at the restaurant was exceptional and represented one of the finest examples of French gastronomy.

The wine list was extensive - one of the best in the world.

The two friends celebrated their return to France by indulging themselves with a rare bottle of 1945 Chateau Petrus, a miraculous vintage that coincided with the end of the war and the same year as the large format bottle of Chateau Mouton-Rothschild which was the prize for their wager.

The sensory confluence of the excellent cuisine and ethereal wine was sublime.

After dinner, they went for a leisurely stroll along the picturesque waterfront.

Invigorated by the sights and sounds of the harbor, they looked forward to hitting the road early the next morning and to seeing their "old friend" Fouquet again very soon!

CHAPTER TEN

The Campaign

As things stood, the two former soldiers agreed that, so far, they were tied.

The *Concorso d'Eleganza Villa d'Este* (*Concours d'Élégance- Villa d'Este*) is one of the preeminent events in the world for classic and vintage cars.

It takes place in Italy on the grounds of the impressive Villa d'Este hotel in Cernobbio along the beautiful shoreline of Lake Como.

This prestigious judging of rare automobiles was first held in 1929 and it is traditionally scheduled every year at the end of May.

Fouquet had bragged to Lockwood, Dunning and Collins at the Pebble Beach show that he would be displaying his Delahaye at Villa d'Este, where the more discerning European judges would be sure to award it the first prize!

With the intention to resoundingly defeat Fouquet at Villa d'Este and to win his wager with Dunning, as well as to secure the *Coppa d'Oro Villa d'Este* (best of show award), Lockwood announced that at great expense he had acquired a pristine original 1954 aluminum-bodied Talbot-Lago T14 LS Coupé.

This rare motorcar had been the Talbot-Lago *Salon-de-L'Automobile-de-Paris* show car.

It featured styling by *Carrosserie Letourneur et Marchand* and an in-house developed 2.5-liter four-cylinder engine with twin laterally mounted camshafts upgraded with five main bearings.

This specification was noteworthy as the marque's final self-developed engine before they sacrilegiously switched to (more reliable) German BMW motors in 1957.

The Villa d'Este show would be an optimum opportunity for Lockwood to spring a trap on the pompous Fouquet in front of all his aristocratic peers!

CHAPTER ELEVEN

The Strike

Colonel Guillaume Fouquet had a trim, almost gaunt physique.

Due, no doubt, not to an ascetic lifestyle, since he was privileged and self-indulgent, but from regular exercise riding and training several horses each day.

Somewhat short in stature, he tended to

undulate as he walked about, almost on tiptoe, as if to exaggerate his somewhat diminutive height.

He affected a cavalry bearing to his posture and was often uniformed in his military tunic which was adorned with the gold epaulettes of his rank.

He habitually carried a riding crop tucked under his arm which he vigorously waved through the air to emphasize his verbal declarations as he strutted about in his tall highly polished riding boots.

Lockwood's tactics to discomfort Fouquet at Villa d'Este involved several stages - both overt, and covert.

Seeing the two Americans again, especially so soon after his embarrassment at Pebble Beach was sure to cause Fouquet consternation!

When Fouquet realized that Lockwood was competing against him in the concours with such a significant motorcar, his anxiety would increase even more!

The culmination of Lockwood's strategy was the installation of a miniature remote kill switch hidden within the electrical system of Fouquet's Delahaye.

When the concours judge requested that Fouquet start the engine of his car to verify its operational status, Lockwood's mischief would cause the car to first misfire and then stall completely…

Then Fouquet would be unable to start the car at all until after the judge had departed.

But even the most meticulous plans can go awry and as things transpired the course of events did not evolve how either Fouquet or Lockwood had expected.

Fouquet was indeed nonplussed upon spotting the Americans as they drove up and he scowled at their Talbot-Lago.

But they were all caught by surprise when a magnificent Bugatti followed them onto the field a few moments afterward.

The 1950s marked the end of a golden age for French motorcar manufacturers.

The last vestige of the era when French automotive designs were regarded as some of the most beautiful and technologically advanced in the world.

At the 1956 Villa d'Este exhibition, three of the greatest French marques - Delahaye, Talbot-Lago and Bugatti were now well represented.

Automobiles Ettore Bugatti had been based in the city of Molsheim in the region of Alsace-Lorraine, which was originally part of the German Empire.

Their elegant styling and painstaking finishing details were regarded as the epitome of automotive design.

After World War I, Alsace was annexed into France and from that point Bugatti was considered a French company.

The German army captured Alsace in World War II and the territory was under their direct rule until the end of the war, even though other parts of France were nominally under the puppet Vichy government control.

During World War II, the Bugatti factory was destroyed and despite plans to resurrect the brand after the war in a new facility outside of Paris, only a handful of cars were built before production stopped in 1952.

There was a subsequent failed attempt to resurrect the company under the auspices of Ettore's son Roland Bugatti, who was an engineer.

The last gasp for the brand was their one-off Type 251 open cockpit single seat race car which was completed in 1955 and featured an inline eight-cylinder motor designed by Gioacchino Colombo.

Columbo was an Italian engineer, best known for the twelve-cylinder Ferrari motors that bore his name.

This rare prototype 251 model was the car that had just pulled up onto the field behind Lockwood and his Talbot-Lago.

Two months after the Villa d'Este Concours, this 251 would be unsuccessfully competed in the French Grand Prix and soon after that Bugatti automobile production would again cease.

After the demise of the motorcar portion of their business, the company remained open for a brief time and continued to manufacture airplane parts.

The marque was eventually sold to Hispano-Suiza in 1963, another former automaker that had repurposed as an aircraft supplier.

The driver of the Bugatti was a silver-haired gentleman who wore steel-rimmed spectacles and was dressed in a doe-skin jacket with a silk scarf.

Dunning noticed Fouquet gazing intently at this new arrival with a very troubled look on his countenance…

The stranger nonchalantly parked the car and proceeded to head off towards the villa without so much as a glance in their direction…

Fouquet approached Lockwood and Dunning and they expected to be treated to some of his usual caustic invective.

Instead, they were taken aback when with a most serious look in his eyes Fouquet asked if they realized who the new arrival was?

Upon seeing their blank expressions, Fouquet proceeded to explain that the man's name was Albert Claden.

According to Fouquet, Claden had been a Nazi collaborator when the Germans invaded Alsace in World War II.

Claden had used labor from the nearby Natzweiler-Struthof concentration camp in the Vosges mountains to work in his factory which supplied automotive parts to the Wehrmacht war industry.

Many of these workers had been prisoners from the resistance movements in German-occupied territories.

When the Germans needed to relocate these inmates to their camp at Dachau because of the approach of Allied forces, Claden had not just turned a blind eye to their deportation.

He had taken an active role in facilitating their transfer even though he knew that this was their death sentence.

Since the war, he had become a recluse and rarely appeared in public.

His despicable role throughout the conflict had quickly been extirpated from public records and conveniently forgotten by influential local officials and inhabitants, many of whom were eager to put their own actions during the occupation behind them…

However, a group of the former Free French Forces officers, including Fouquet, had been working to identify and track down former Vichy and Alsace collaborators who they viewed as war criminals.

Many of the worst offenders, like Claden, had proved to be very elusive…

Now, however, evidently the opportunity to display his rare Bugatti at Villa d'Este had caused Claden to make an exception to his policy of solitude and tempted him out of his lair…

Fouquet formally requested a commitment from Lockwood and Dunning to assist him with apprehending Claden so that he could bring this evil villain back to France to stand trial for the atrocities he had participated in.

For all his faults and character flaws, Fouquet had been a distinguished military officer and had served his country honorably during the war.

Though this would undoubtably be an uneasy alliance and certainly not undertaken by their preference, out of a shared military warrior ethos the two American veterans quietly nodded their agreement.

CHAPTER TWELVE

The Alliance

The conspirators were well-aware that what they were contemplating was very dicey.

They would be operating illegally on Italian soil and if they were caught they would be subject to kidnapping charges, with no government infrastructure to rescue them or negotiate their release.

The window of opportunity was very time sensitive with only a few hours to formulate and execute their scheme.

Dunning suggested a diversion that immediately appealed to Lockwood.

Fouquet brooded about the proposal as he smoked a *Gauloises Disque Bleu* cigarette.

To the Americans' surprise, Fouquette assented, acknowledging their greater experience with furtive activities.

The key to success would be to challenge Claden's ego by appealing to his sense of French national pride, which, as someone from Alsace, he would likely be inclined to emphasize given the checkered history of that region.

The Alsace region is famed for their *eau-de-vie* clear brandies distilled from local fruits.

These high alcohol spirits which are quite potent can quickly incapacitate an unwary imbiber.

The Italian equivalent, made from

grapes, is called *grappa* and it is traditionally produced in the northern regions of the country.

Much would depend on how Claden had been spending his time in self-imposed isolation since the war.

Would feelings of guilt for his crimes, combined with constant fear of retribution have caused him to regularly drink to excess?

Dunning went to the villa to find a member of the event staff who could assist him with quickly acquiring a selection of *grappas*.

Fouquet and Lockwood went in search of Claden, with the intention to engage him in conversation about his Bugatti and about the auto parts that he manufactured.

As soon as Dunning returned with the *grappas*, they would suggest that Claden join them for a drink to help while away the afternoon as the laborious process of the judging was conducted.

CHAPTER THIRTEEN

The Ploy

Lockwood and Fouquet found Claden examining a 1949 Ferrari 166 *Mille Miglia Barchetta "Panoramica,"*, which had initially been built by Zagato as a *Coupé* and then rebodied a year later as a *Spyder*.

They engaged him in conversation by suggesting that his Bugatti was a much more beautiful design.

The ruse worked and Claden spent the next ten minutes explaining to his new audience why no other automobile could compare with Bugatti's level of elegant mechanical and aesthetic craftsmanship.

Lockwood and Fouquet further indulged Claden's sense of self-importance by observing that while their Delahaye and Talbot-Lago were two of the finest French motorcars, they could not compete with Claden's exquisite Bugatti which would surely win the best of show honor.

As the three men were agreeing that French automotive designs were clearly superior to those from the Italians and the British, Dunning arrived with a selection of twelve *grappas* and snifters to taste them.

They invited Claden to join them for their *dégustation*, suggesting that the objective of the exercise was to disprove the local claim that *grappa* was superior to the *eau-de-vies* made in Alsace.

As they had surmised, Claden was just as ardent about Alsace spirits as he was about Bugatti and other indigenous products.

Fouquet suggested that while they could not actually compare and contrast, since they did not have any Alsace *eau-de-vie* with them to sample, they could still fully disprove the fallacy of *grappa's* supremacy with a tasting and discussion about all twelve varieties.

This thorough procedure to verify the primacy of Alsace brandies appealed to Claden's detail-oriented sensibility.

Dunning had brought some local cheeses and cured meats to enjoy with the tasting.

Feigning insomnia, he had also prevailed on the staff to give him some *Nembutal*, which combined with the effects from the alcohol would knock out Claden for a sufficient length of time for them to be able to transport him to France where Fouquet's colleagues would be able to legally detain him.

CHAPTER FOURTEEN

The Escape

They began with a *grappa* that, according to the label, was made primarily from Picolit grapes.

The fiery spirit burned as it went down with immediate effects that were almost disorienting.

Claden alleged that the quality of the

various local fruits was what most differentiated Alsace spirits from these rustic Italian *grappas*.

He claimed that the delicate white Alsace peaches and the intense flavor of their local blackberries were excellent examples of the purity of flavor exhibited in their spirits, as opposed to these overpowering Italian grape brandies which assaulted the senses.

They proceeded to sample another *grappa* from a different producer with much the same consensus.

Dunning had succeeded to mix some of the drug into Claden's portion without him noticing.

The tasting process continued for the next half hour until Claden, of a sudden, began slurring his words and looking disoriented...

Lockwood suggested to Claden that he relax for a few minutes in the Talbot-Lago which had a more spacious interior then the Bugati.

By the time Lockwood and Dunning

had settled Claden into the car, he was unconscious.

Swiftly, they conferred with Fouquet and decided to make a run for it.

Lockwood would drive Claden in the Talbot-Lago, with Fouquet following in the Delahaye and Dunning would drive the Bugati.

To the amazed looks of the judges and spectators, they fired up the engines and swiftly departed the show grounds.

The three stunning French motorcars made quite a spectacle as they roared down the driveway…

CHAPTER FIFTEEN

The Chase

A security car began to follow them, until the driver's attention was distracted by the explosion of a 1950 Maserati A6 1500 which Dunning had rigged as their diversion.

With luck, their journey of four-hundred and seventy *kilometres* to meet one of Fouquet's compatriots in Lyon should take them approximately five and a half hours to complete.

Once they arrived at the French border, they should be safe…

Fouquet's travel documents, which identified him as a former high-ranking army officer, should suffice to get them expedited across.

But their journey would not be as uneventful as they had hoped…

One of the organizers of the concours was concerned by the unexplained and hasty departure of three of the most talked about entrants.

He became alarmed when the Maserati exploded and instead of calling the local *Polizia* to investigate, he phoned the *Carabinieri* military police station instead, who, given the important status of the caller, immediately dispatched a car to search for them and sent their other three units to Villa d'Este to investigate the explosion.

The officer charged to investigate the

sudden departure of the concours entrants succeeded to find them, but his vehicle was no match for the handling prowess of the three race cars as they navigated the twisty lanes along the picturesque lakeshore.

However, top speed for the fugitives was limited by these same secondary roads.

They needed to get onto the motorway as quickly as possible, where their superior speed would allow them to escape pursuit.

As they traversed their escape route, they encountered all manner of cumbersome trucks and slow-moving cars.

The French cars were pushed to the limits of their handling and acceleration as the drivers aggressively passed obstructing traffic.

During one passing maneuver, the three cars barely succeeded to get around a truck without being hit by an oncoming bus.

The Carabinieri officer did not fare so well, running head-on into the approaching coach.

The impromptu kidnappers could only hope that the officer had not had time to radio into his station before crashing and that they would not encounter additional run-ins with the authorities.

When they reached the highway, they pushed the accelerators to the floorboards and released the full potential of the amazing machines.

Children in vehicles that they passed pointed in wonder, while less impressionable adults frowned in disapproval.

The fugitives stopped for fuel outside of Turin, nervously watching for signs of pursuit…

At the border, as Fouquet spoke to the customs agents the two Americans breathed a collective sigh of relief…

When they arrived at their destination in Lyon, Fouquet rang the bell at an impressive *maison*.

The man who opened the door spoke briefly with Fouquet, then assisted him with carrying Claden inside.

Fouquet came back to Lockwood and Dunning just long enough to instruct them to leave the Bugati and to depart immediately!

Reverting to his old insolent demeanor, he neglected to thank them before returning to the house and shutting the door behind him…

EPILOGUE

The Aftermath

During this brief sabbatical, Lockwood and Dunning had succeeded to recapture some of the excitement of their former glory days in the army.

An unexpected result of what had transpired over the course of this adventure was that they now had a grudging respect for the insufferable Fouquet!

Some of the scenery in the European regions they had revisited reminded them of their erstwhile escapades.

Other places were no longer recognizable and they realized that given the grim events and bloody battles which had taken place in those locations during the war, that the change was for the best.

The same organizational skills and tactics that they had learned during their military service, which had helped them hone their ability to create successful businesses in civilian life, had yet again been effective to achieve their objectives and navigate the unforeseen "twists and turns in the road" that had forced them to reassess their plans on the fly.

The adventure had motivated and challenged them and would provide cherished memories for many years to come.

As they had always privately known would be the outcome, the two friends imbibed the magnum of 1945 Chateau Mouton-Rothschild together.

They had their waiter bring extra glasses so they could share this special wine with other diners in the restaurant; complete strangers who were astonished at their largesse!

The realization that a wine of this legendary caliber had been made during the severe strife and hardships in the final year of the war, was almost as profound as acknowledging their good fortune to have survived that hellacious conflict.

An attribute of the greatest wines is that they stimulate, not just the palate, but also the mind, inspiring animated thoughts and conversation that lead to insights and contemplation.

As they explored the nuances of bouquet and flavor, the two old friends reflected on their shared experiences over the past several months.

They realized that not since the war ended had they felt so energized and completely alive, and they toasted their good fortune with the sublime 1945 Chateau Mouton-Rothschild!

Please enjoy the prologue of
Derailed Gears

PROLOGUE

(In cycling, a prologue is a short preliminary time trial
held before a race to establish a leader)

L ate one night, Ernesto Sante was laboring in his small makeshift workshop, to finish building a custom lightweight steel racing bicycle frame, for famed local racer—Gino Fausto, the favorite to win the upcoming prestigious *Giro d'Italia* competition.

Sante, who had been nicknamed The Tailor by the European racing community, was a legendary builder.

He possessed extraordinary skill at creating short wheelbase racing frames, with stiff, catlike handling, that, due to the meticulous bespoke measurements for the rider's physique, were surprisingly comfortable to ride over long distances.

An important attribute for grueling races such as the *Giro*.

He was a true craftsman, and his frames not only consistently performed well, but were also beautiful to behold.

Unlike the famed French *constructeurs*, who, in the 1950s, were for the most part focused on building filet-brazed lugless touring bicycles, with elaborate braze-ons to attach proprietary components- for racing bikes, Italian frames had become the preferred choice amongst many top competitors, and Sante was recognized as one of the elite artisans.

Sante favored bright colors for his frames, devoid of pinstriping and contrasting panels, to highlight his signature Florentine *fleur-de-lis* cutouts, which he engraved by hand in the minimalist hand-shaped, and painstakingly filed and finished lugs, with elegant shorelines.

His detailing, was much subtler than the complex embellishments favored by many British frame makers at that time, which resembled the elaborate curvilinear designs of fine sterling silver culinary utensils, and intricately engraved bespoke shotgun sideplates.

Sante's brazing technique, included the use of both bronze rod for the thicker metal of bottom brackets and dropouts, and nickel silver for the much thinner-walled lug joinery.

Most Italian builders used domestically made Columbus tubing, exclusively for their projects, but Sante always combined a proprietary mix of both Columbus, and British Reynolds tubing for each build, specifically chosen for each rider's physique, and the intended use for the frame.

He eschewed using a frame jig, which he felt placed unwanted stress on the tubing, and could cause subsequent warping and hairline cracks.

He preferred to build completely by eye, constantly checking trueness against the hand drawn plans he custom designed for each client.

When it was time to proceed with the brazing, he turned on his oxyacetylene tanks, and lighting the torch, he adjusted the flow of the gasses.

He further fine-tuned the combination of oxygen, and acetylene to create optimum inner and outer envelopes of flame.

As he began to heat the area where the chainstays were inserted into the bottom bracket, he was disturbed to hear an unusual hissing sound emanating from the area where the gas tanks were standing.

In all his years of brazing, he had never discerned such a sound before...

Irritated, because the bottom bracket

had now reached the perfect shade of cherry red to begin filling in the voids with the bronze rod, he pulled back from his work to look at the tanks and hoses, to determine what was causing the discordant sound.

As he turned with torch in hand, he was aghast, to hear, and see, the roar of an ignited conflagration, and feel a concussive explosion.

These were the final impressions in the fading conscious of The Tailor…

ABOUT THE AUTHOR

E. Robert Brooks writes historical fiction mystery stories, that feature topics such as- fine wine, equestrian competition, bicycle racing, and vintage motorcars.

He is a longtime car enthusiast and has participated in track days at several acclaimed racecourses, and has driven in vintage road rallies in America, and Europe.

As a collector, he has restored notable grand touring automobiles, and sportscars, including- a 1958 Facel Vega HK500, a

1965 Alfa Romeo Giulia Sprint Speciale, 1959 and 1960 MGA LeMans tributes, a 1961 Bentley S2, and a 1969 MGB hotrod race car.

His Mother was the noted journalist-Jane Gregory Brooks.